WHO LIKES IT HOT ?

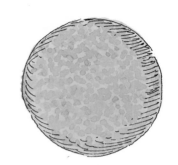

For Tess, who prefers it hot—J.O'B

The pictures are drawn with a rapidograph pen on Strathmore Bristol Board and then
painted using condensed water colors and dyes.

Text copyright © 1972 by May Garelick
Illustrations copyright © 1998 by John O'Brien

For information contact:
MONDO Publishing
One Plaza Road
Greenvale, New York 11548
Visit our web site at www.mondopub.com

Printed in Hong Kong
98 99 00 01 02 03 04   HC   9 8 7 6 5 4 3 2 1
98 99 00 01 02 03 04   PB   9 8 7 6 5 4 3 2 1

Designed by Sylvia Frezzolini Severance
Production by The Kids at Our House

Library of Congress Cataloging-in-Publication Data
Garelick, May.
   Who likes it hot? / by May Garelick ; illustrated by John O'Brien.
         p.   cm.
   Summary: Explains, in rhymed text and illustrations, why certain animals
prefer hot climates and others prefer cold.
      ISBN 1-57255-553-X (alk. paper). — ISBN 1-57255-554-8 (pbk. : alk. paper)
   [1. Animals—Fiction.   2. Stories in rhyme.]   I. O'Brien, John, ill.   II. Title.
      PZ8.3.G18Wh   1998
      [E]—dc21   97-32713
                                                                          CIP
                                                                           AC

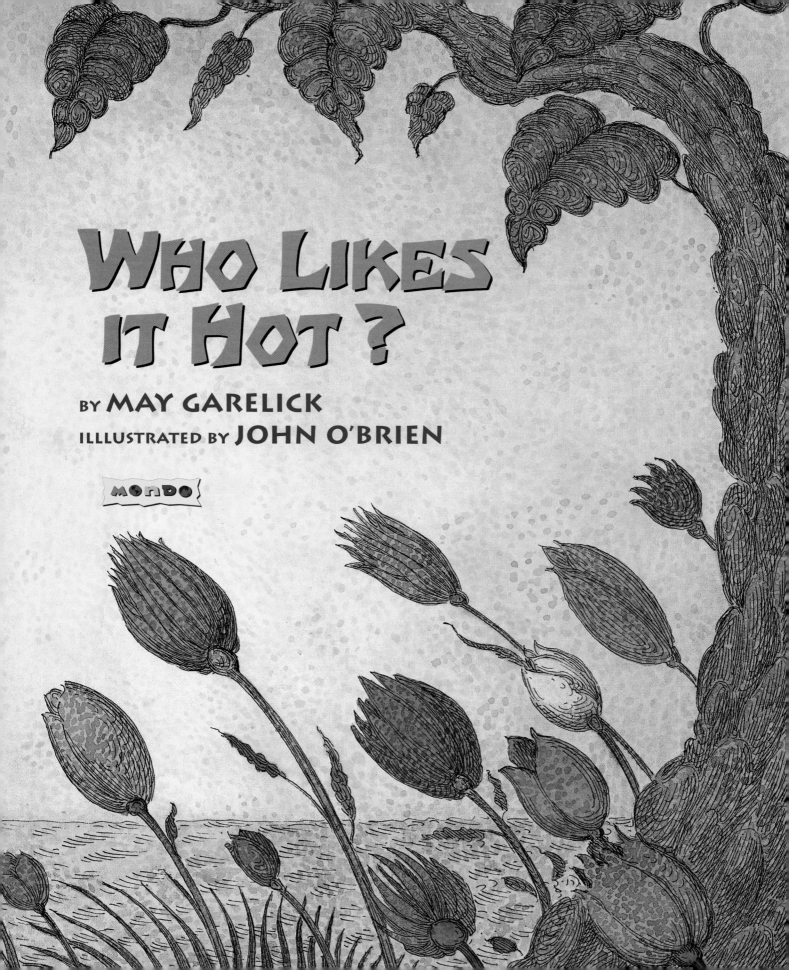

WHO LIKES IT HOT?

BY **MAY GARELICK**

ILLLUSTRATED BY **JOHN O'BRIEN**

MONDO

Birds calling.
Worms crawling.
Bugs hopping.
Buds popping.
End of spring.

Summer is here.

It's hot.

Some like it.

Some do not.

Who likes it hot?

Birds seem to like it hot.

And why not?

Pick   Peck   Cheep   Tweet

So many things for a bird to eat.

Berries, cherries, worms, and seeds,

everything that any bird needs.

Pick   Peck   Cheep   Tweet

Birds don't seem to mind the heat.

And there's no doubt about
a mosquito.
You know when it's best
for that pest!
When it's hot,
you swat.

Mosquitoes, bees, flies, and fleas.
When it's hot
there are plenty of these.
Insects like it hot.

Does a frog
like it hot?
Sometimes yes, sometimes not.
A frog is in a wonderful spot.
When the sun gets hot
on a frog's thin skin,
plunk—into the water
it dives for a swim.

A snake will bake
in the blazing sun.
But this reptile's not the only one.
Lizards bake, too.
But even they
can't take a bake
in the sun all day.
When snakes and lizards get too hot,
they slither and slide
to a cooler spot.

They cool off in the shade, and then come back out in the sun again. Reptiles like it hot.

What about mammals?
Do they like it hot?
Some do. Some do not.

A camel is one mammal
that's hard to persuade
to stay in the shade.
A camel is made to withstand
burning sun and sand.

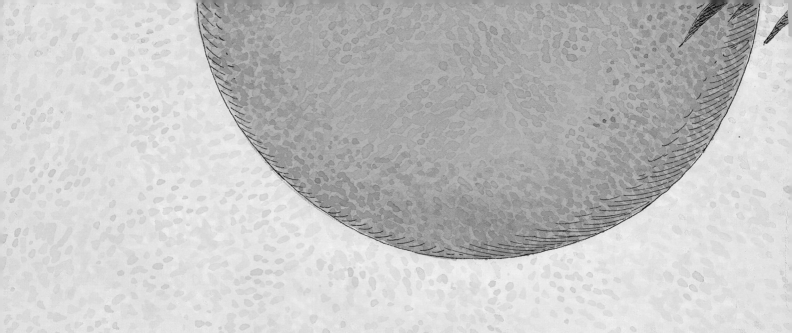

But a polar bear could not stand
hot desert sun and sand.
It would die
if the temperature
went too high.

The walrus and the Arctic hare,
the fur seal and the polar bear
live in lands of ice and snow
where temperatures go very low.
They do not
like it hot.

Oops! There's another one
I nearly forgot.
A ptarmigan doesn't like it hot.

All creatures live
where it suits them best.
Where they find food.
Where they find rest.

That's why
you'll never see
a lizard
in a blizzard.
Or a parakeet flitting
where a polar bear is sitting.

You won't find a camel
on a block of ice.
But for a fur seal,
ice is nice.

What about you?
Could you live where
there's ice and snow?

Yes!
There's no place
you can't go.
Where it's cold
or where it's hot,
you can live
in any spot.